# BABAR'S
## BIRTHDAY
## SURPRISE

# BABAR'S
## BIRTHDAY
## SURPRISE

**LAURENT DE BRUNHOFF**

Abrams Books for Young Readers, New York

The artist Podular was making a sculpture of Babar, the king of the elephants. Queen Celeste, Cousin Arthur, and the Old Lady were amazed at how much the little statue looked like Babar.

At the end of the session, Celeste spoke to Podular.
"I want you to carve a whole mountain to look like Babar.
As a birthday surprise," she said. "Can you do that?"
   The sculptor said yes.

"It's a surprise," Celeste reminded him. "So you must keep the work secret."

"I'll do my best," replied Podular. "But hiding a mountain won't be easy."

With the help of Zephir the monkey, Podular loaded his truck and headed out of town.

They found a spot where the stone was good for carving and cut down some trees to make scaffolding.

Two marabous wanted to help.

"I could use lookouts," said Podular. "We want this to be a surprise."

But before the birds could even take to the air, Zephir cried, "Babar is coming on his bicycle!"

Babar often took this road to go fishing. Fortunately,
he was not looking around, and he seemed to notice nothing.
    But the marabous could see how
much Podular needed their help.
They found a giraffe to work
as a lookout, too.

Podular went to work carving Babar's crown. Then he started drilling the face.

"Look out!" cried the giraffe. "Someone's coming in a red car!"

Podular knew the red car belonged to Cousin Arthur, and he wasn't worried. "Come watch as I work," Podular said to Arthur, "but don't get in the way, and keep this a secret. It's supposed to be a surprise."

The head of the statue was soon finished.
Podular started to work on the body.
    The marabous started squawking,
"Someone else is coming!"

This time it was Babar's children—Pom, Flora, and Alexander.

"You are welcome to watch," said Podular. "But don't tell anyone, because we want this to be a surprise."

Soon Podular was working on the feet. He was almost finished with the statue.

"Time for a picnic!" cried the children.

Back in Celesteville, everyone was working on Babar's birthday celebration. Poutifour the gardener was growing flowers for the table.

The cooks and the Old Lady were working on a cake.

Celeste took Babar for a walk. She could tell something was on his mind. She wondered if he suspected anything. But he didn't. He was upset because he had lost his favorite pipe when he went fishing.

Meanwhile, Cornelius rehearsed the band for their performance on the big day.

Later, on the mountain, the picnic was over and the children were playing when once again the marabous and the giraffe gave the alarm.

Babar was coming on his bicycle!

He was looking for his pipe, he told the giraffe.
Just then Flora, hiding behind the bushes,
happened to step on the pipe. The marabous flew
over and grabbed it.

"Here is your pipe," said one of the marabous. "But I'm afraid it's broken."

"No matter," said Babar. "I can glue it together." And he headed back to Celesteville without noticing the sculpture.

The children were so happy the surprise wasn't ruined that they jumped up and down on the scaffolding.

"Stop that!" said Podular. But it was too late. A board came loose, and the whole scaffolding collapsed.

Arthur sprained his trunk in the fall. Zephir quickly drove the red car to Celesteville and brought back Dr. Capoulosse.

Dr. Capoulosse bandaged Arthur's trunk and said the sprain wasn't serious.

"But, Doctor, will you keep the work here secret?" asked Arthur. "It is supposed to be a surprise."

"Of course," said the doctor. He then took them back to town.

Now Podular had to figure out how to wrap the statue to keep it hidden until the right moment—the hardest job of all. He consulted the marabous about what to do.

The next day a crowd came from Celesteville. Celeste had invited everyone to a concert at the foot of the mountain, with lunch to follow.

Millions of birds covered the side of the mountain.
   "Are they here for the concert, too?" Babar asked.
   "Yes," Celeste answered. "Everyone wants to celebrate your birthday!"

The band, led by Cornelius, struck up a fanfare.
At this signal, the birds covering the mountain all
flew away at the same time.

The gigantic statue of Babar was revealed. Everyone was astonished, especially Babar.

"This is the best birthday I've ever had," said Babar. "And what a surprise! Thank you all so much. I can only imagine how hard you've worked to arrange this. Thank you most of all, Podular."

But Podular, tired from his labor, was already asleep.

The artwork for each picture is prepared using watercolor on paper.
This text is set in 16-point Comic Sans.

The Library of Congress has cataloged the original Abrams edition of this book as follows:

Library of Congress Cataloging-in-Publication Data

Brunhoff, Laurent de.
    [Anniversaire de Babar. English]
    Babar's Birthday Surprise / Laurent de Brunhoff.
        p. cm.
Summary: Queen Celeste decides to surprise King Babar with a statue of himself for his birthday but has a diffiult time keeping it a secret.
    ISBN 0-8109-5713-2
    [1. Elephants—Fiction.] I. Title.

PZ7.B82843 Babiu 2002
[E]—dc21                                        2001003741

ISBN for this edition: 978-1-4197-0383-6

Printed and bound in China
10 9 8 7 6 5 4 3 2

Abrams Books for Young Readers are available at special discounts when purchased in quantity for premiums and promotions as well as fundraising or educational use. Special editions can also be created to specification. For details, contact specialsales@abramsbooks.com or the address below.

ABRAMS
THE ART OF BOOKS SINCE 1949

115 West 18th Street
New York, NY 10011
www.abramsbooks.com